animal
lovers

Full of
Christmassy
magic

Lovely
illustrations

A
Magic Snow
Globe!

Make
a wish!

LC
9/17

Here's the moment Lucy meets Pixie the donkey for the first time . . .

Pixie was a very gentle animal. She came slowly towards the girls and let them pat her neck. She bent her head and Lucy felt her soft ears. Then the girls let her out into the field whilst they cleared out the dirty straw from the stable and put some fresh hay in the manger, some donkey pellets in the feeding trough, and clean water in the water bucket.

Pixie took her time to come back in, and she had a bit of mud on her back when she did. 'She loves rolling on the ground,' said Rosie. 'But she does get in a mess.'

Pixie wasn't interested in eating the new hay. She let Rosie gently brush the mud away but then walked off, as if to say, 'That's enough.'

To Nieve Muir and Sarah Broadley—
reading buddies who shared a Lucy
book—I hope you like this one—and
notice the vet's name!

And to Connie Jones from
Pontypridd, who loves animals.

OXFORD
UNIVERSITY PRESS

Great Clarendon Street, Oxford OX2 6DP
Oxford University Press is a department of the University of Oxford.
It furthers the University's objective of excellence in research, scholarship,
and education by publishing worldwide. Oxford is a registered trade mark of
Oxford University Press in the UK and in certain other countries

British Library Cataloguing in Publication Data
Data available
ISBN: 9780192749802

1 3 5 7 9 10 8 6 4 2

Printed in Great Britain
Paper used in the production of this book is a natural,
recyclable product made from wood grown in sustainable forests.
The manufacturing process conforms to the environmental
regulations of the country of origin.

LUCY'S MAGICAL
SURPRISE

Written by Anne Booth
Illustrated by Sophy Williams

OXFORD
UNIVERSITY PRESS

Chapter One

It was the first afternoon of the Christmas holidays. Lucy and her friends, Rosie and Sita, were helping out at Lucy's Gran's Wildlife Rescue Centre, cleaning out the cages. It was hard work, but it was good to know that all the animals that were there—six little hedgehogs, a squirrel with a bad foot, and a blackbird with a broken wing—would be comfortable and clean. Lucy helped her Gran out every weekend all year round, and she even had a special red sweatshirt she wore as her uniform. She was very proud to wear it today as she showed her best friends what to do.

'I love all the badges your Gran has made for your uniform,' said Sita. 'One for every type of animal you have helped. I remember the first one she made you for little Bub, the rabbit, the Christmas I first came here from Australia.'

'Now you've got a magpie, a newt, a rabbit, and a hedgehog on this arm,' said Rosie.

'And there's a baby otter on this one,' said Lucy. 'I can't believe that was last Christmas. He was very sweet but very naughty! It was so good we found him a place at the otter sanctuary. Gran and I went to see him learning to swim and he made such a lot of noise!'

'I'll have to make you lots more badges for all the animals you've helped this year, Lucy,' said Gran, coming in from the kitchen. 'I'm a bit behind on my embroidery! The trouble is, the wild animals come in faster than I can make badges. I wish they could live in a safer world. But there's not much we can do about that. So we just have to help them as best as we can. And I don't know what I'd do without you, Lucy, I really don't.'

Lucy gave her Gran a big hug. Apart from playing with Sita and Rosie, looking after animals and birds was her favourite thing to do, and she had lots of books about them. She loved reading them in bed, her little cat Merry and her pyjama-case dog Scruffy tucked up beside her, and her rocking horse Rocky looking on.

Gran looked at the clean cages and floor, and smiled at the three friends.

'My goodness, you have all worked

extremely hard today. Thank you so much! Why don't you wash your hands and then sit down and have some juice and the Christmas biscuits Lucy made me.'

The girls came and sat down in Gran's cosy kitchen. She had Christmas

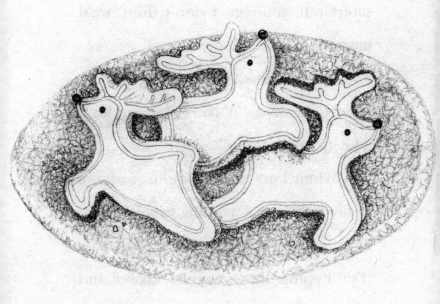

cards and decorations up all over the house, and Christmas carols were playing in the background.

'These are yummy, Lucy!' said Rosie, eating one of the biscuits. 'And I like the reindeer shape!'

'Now, that's a badge you haven't got!' said Gran, smiling. 'I don't think we'd have room for a reindeer here!'

Lucy laughed. 'Oh I don't know, Gran!' she said. 'A baby one wouldn't take up much room!'

'When I go back to live in Australia in the New Year, I'm going to see if I can help out at a wildlife centre,' said Sita. 'I'm hoping there will be koalas and kangaroos there. Maybe I'll even help a joey!'

'What's a joey?' said Lucy.

'It's a baby kangaroo,' said Sita.

'We're going to miss you so much,' said Lucy, suddenly feeling sad. 'I can't believe you are going.'

'I'll miss you too,' said Sita quietly.

'Well, we were lucky to have her and her family for two years,' said Gran. 'And don't forget the puppy Sita is getting in the New Year!'

All the girls brightened up. Ever since they had known Sita was finally going home, they had been talking about the puppy her mum and dad had promised her when they got back to their house in Australia.

'I'll send you lots of pictures!' said Sita. 'I can't wait to collect her—I am going to teach her to sit and fetch and roll over, and we'll go for walks by the beach. She will miss home, the way I did when I came here, but I'll take her to puppy parties and she'll make new friends, like I did you.'

'Hey! We're not puppies!' said Lucy.

'I think it is lovely that your mum and stepdad have moved you all into your grandad's farm, Rosie,' said Gran. 'How exciting that this will be your first Christmas there! Your grandad must be so happy.'

'Yes,' said Rosie. 'When he got ill he couldn't look after it very well, so he is glad we have taken over now. He is coming to stay for Christmas, after the concert at the old people's home.'

'I hope you are singing again this year,' said Gran. 'You have such a lovely voice, Rosie.'

'Yes, I'm singing a carol about a little donkey,' said Rosie.

'And we're seeing Pixie the donkey tomorrow!' said Lucy. 'I can't wait!'

That night Lucy snuggled up in bed and sleepily watched the light from

her Christmas snow globe lamp. She
thought about all the animals she and
Gran had helped in the past year. Lucy

felt sad that so many had been hurt, but glad that they had helped them. Lucy reached over and shook the lamp gently so that the snow fell on the little house in the wood. It was so pretty. She had had it for as long as she could remember, and she always imagined that there was something magic about it, but somehow she didn't know exactly why she thought that. It was as if she had dreamt about it but couldn't recall what was in the dreams.

'I'm sure if any animals live in your wood they are safe and happy,' Lucy said to the snow globe. She settled down in bed, cuddling Scruffy her pyjama case, her little cat Merry purring beside her. Rocky her rocking horse looked down with his kind eyes shining as the moonlight peeped though the curtains, and Lucy closed her eyes and fell fast asleep.

So she didn't see that, for a moment, the snow falling in the globe had turned all the different colours of the rainbow, sparkling blue and red and orange and green and yellow and purple, and there was a distant sound of tinkling bells.

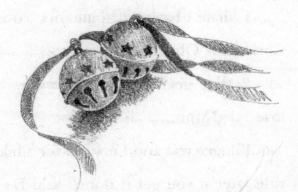

Chapter Two

It was Tuesday of Christmas week. Lucy's dad was whistling Christmas carols and putting up lots of decorations. He was very cheerful because of the Christmas holidays, but Lucy's brother Oscar was a bit grumpy.

'I hate having homework over Christmas,' Oscar said.

'Best to get it over and done with, love,' said Mum.

'I'll take you and Lucy out for a bike ride later if you get it done,' said Dad. 'What is it about?'

'I've got to write about an animal which used to be in this village but isn't any more,' grumbled Oscar. 'I tried to look it up online but our village isn't famous enough. I don't know how to find out what animal it was.'

'Well, I know just the person to ask,' said Dad. 'You can go over to Gran's with Lucy this morning and I am sure she will

14

know. I could almost guess myself but I'll let her tell you.'

'Harvest mice!' said Gran, when Lucy and Oscar went over to her house and asked her. 'We always used to have lots of harvest mice in the fields around here. They are beautiful little creatures.

I'm afraid the way we farm now means that they and lots of other small animals and birds and insects have lost their homes—they need hedges and they need grass to build their nests in, but the fields are ploughed up right to the edges, and too much weedkiller is used. It's such a shame.'

'Thanks, Gran,' said Oscar. He had cheered up being over at Gran's. Oscar spent most of his free time playing football now, but he was very good with animals, and as soon as he had arrived he had gone straight over to talk to the little squirrel with a bad foot. It went up to the bars and sat up and looked at him and chattered back a bit, so it seemed to like him too.

Gran got out some paper and scissors and tape.

'Oscar, have a hot chocolate with me and Lucy, and stay and wrap up the animals' presents,' said Gran.

'Why are you wrapping presents for the animals?' said Oscar. 'They won't notice.' But he smiled and came and sat down anyway, and started wrapping up some nuts for the squirrel. It was cosy and warm, and there was a delicious smell of baking cakes coming from the oven. Gran had put up fairy lights around her kitchen window and they flashed on and off and made the room feel especially Christmassy.

'I like to decorate a Christmas tree for them. I think the animals are part of the Christmas story too—look at how important the donkey was!' said Gran.

'I love donkeys!' said Lucy. 'I'm going to see Pixie tomorrow morning. I'm going for a sleepover tonight at Rosie's grandad's farm.'

'I'm so glad that Rosie's mum said that they could look after a rescue donkey for a few weeks, especially with Pixie being pregnant,' said Gran. 'It is so sad that my friend's animal shelter had to close down, and I just don't have room to look after donkeys the way he did. I'm sure Rosie's grandad is pleased to hear there is a donkey on his farm again. I'm going to pop over and see him in the home now.'

'Shall I come with you?' said Lucy. She loved Rosie's grandad. He always had so many stories to tell about growing up in the countryside and the animals he used to see.

'That would be lovely, Lucy,' said Gran. 'He is feeling very sad about the farm. He is missing it and worrying about how Rosie's mum and Peter are going to fix all the things that have gone wrong this past year. It needs such a lot of money to keep going.'

'Are you going to bring him over some cake?' said Oscar, looking hungry.

Gran laughed and took the fairy cakes out of the oven. She put them on the baking rack to cool. They looked so good. 'Yes, but don't worry—I've made some for you to bring home too, and there's enough to bring over to Rosie's if you like, Lucy. Now, we'll hang these treats up on the Christmas tree. Thank you both so much for your help!'

'And thanks for telling me about the harvest mice,' said Oscar. 'Now I know what animal it was I can look it up and write about it. Look—I've found a picture of one on my phone.'

Oscar showed Lucy and Gran the picture on his phone. It was of a very tiny mouse balancing between two blades of grass, and another on some wheat.

'That's called an ear of wheat,' said Gran. 'Can you imagine how tiny a harvest mouse is? It is the tiniest mouse we have!'

'It is so sweet!' said Lucy. 'I wish I could see one!'

'So do I,' said Gran. 'I'm sad to think you won't see the animals I did when I was growing up. That's why I'm trying to look after the wild ones we already have.'

'Thanks again, Gran,' said Oscar, taking the box of still-warm cakes.

'I'll see you at home, Lucy. If I get my homework written up, Dad will take us for a bike ride after lunch.'

Gran and Lucy went to Forest Lodge, where Rosie's grandad was living. He was very pleased with Gran's cakes.

'I'll have one as a treat later,' he said. 'What are you up to, Lucy?' His eyes twinkled at her and Lucy smiled back.

'I'm going for a sleepover at the farm,' said Lucy. 'I can't wait to see Pixie the donkey.'

'Thank you for saying that we could keep Pixie in your barn,' said Gran. 'It was such a help and we can keep a close eye on her there.'

'Oh, I'm very happy to think of an animal back on the farm, and that Rosie and Leah can see her. We had so many animals when I was young—hens, ducks, goats, sheep, and donkeys. It just makes me sad to think of the farm going to waste the way it has,' sighed Rosie's grandad. 'I do miss it. This is a very nice home, but I am looking forward to spending

Christmas back at the farm.'

'And everyone is looking forward to seeing you back there, I know,' said Gran, giving him a hug. 'We'll get you back on that piano and you can sing us a few Christmas carols!'

'I'm looking forward to that!' laughed Rosie's grandad. 'Thanks for popping by—you've really cheered me up!'

When Lucy got home Mum had made some delicious soup and fresh bread for lunch.

'I love holidays!' she said. 'I love my job, but I so enjoy having the time to cook.'

'And I like having the time to eat your wonderful food!' said Dad, winking at Lucy. 'Although I must say that I have some special meals planned too—my famous curry, and my roast potatoes and stuffing for Christmas lunch when Prajit and Joanna and Sita come over for their last Christmas here. I want to make it special for them.'

Mum, Lucy, Oscar, and Dad went for a bike ride after lunch. It was fun cycling out in the cold winter air, and Lucy loved it when they got away from the traffic and on to the quieter country lanes, past the sheep fields. A blackbird sang and flew low across the road as they cycled past, and Lucy could almost imagine there were no cars and that they lived in a time when people used horses and carts—or donkeys and carts—to get about.

When they got home, Lucy went up to her room and packed her overnight bag.

'Merry, you can keep Rocky company,' she said to her little cat, who was curled up half asleep on the bed. Merry rolled over and stretched so that Lucy could rub her furry tummy. 'I wish I could take you with me, Rocky, but Scruffy is the only one who will fit in my bag. Maybe I'll take the snow globe too. I've never had a sleepover at the farm before, and I think Rosie's house might be very dark at night so I might like to see it glowing. I've got a funny feeling inside that I'm going to have an adventure and, if I'm going to have an adventure, I'll need my special snow globe with me!'

Chapter Three

Mum dropped Lucy off at Rosie's grandad's farm. It was a big, old farmhouse down a country lane. It was cold and dark when they got there but the sky was clear, and there were lots of stars. There was also a special smell in

the air as they walked up the dark path
to the door.

'They must have an open fire,' said
Lucy's mum. 'How lovely!'

'Come in!' said Rosie's mum to
Lucy's mum, and brought them into the
big farmhouse kitchen.

The long red velvet curtains were
faded and the paint on the walls was a
bit chipped and the rugs were worn, but
it was colourful and welcoming. There
was a big wooden dresser with different
patterned mugs and plates, a fireplace
with burning logs, a big table, and there
were lots of bright paper chains hanging
across the room. Sita and Rosie were

sitting at the table making more paper chains with Leah, Rosie's little sister. Leah was very excited about the big girls coming, and had been allowed to stay up late to see them. She was perched on lots of cushions so she could reach the table, and she was wearing a hairband with a little pair of ears, and her face was painted with a little brown nose and whiskers.

'What are you, Leah?' said Lucy, sitting next to her and giving the little girl a hug.

'I'm a little mouse!' said Leah, 'Eek! Eek!'

'They had face painting at the

Christmas party at Leah's nursery today,' said Rosie, 'and Leah has been pretending to be a mouse all evening.'

'I heard about a very, very little mouse today,' said Lucy to Leah. 'I saw a picture of it on Oscar's phone. It was so tiny it could balance on a blade of grass!'

'I want to see one!' said Leah.

'We can look for one tomorrow,' said Rosie firmly. 'Little mice are asleep now. You can help us with the paper chains.'

'What a wonderful old house!' said Lucy's mum to Rosie's mum as the girls made the paper chains.

'Yes,' replied Rosie's mum. 'It is beautiful. The real worry is the land. The fields are overgrown and we don't have the money to fix the machinery we need to use. It's all a mess. I thought we could put things right, but now we've moved in I'm not so sure we can. I really don't even know if we can stay here. To buy all the weedkiller and machinery and clear the ground all costs so much money and takes so much time.'

'What a shame,' said Lucy's mum, and gave Rosie's mum a hug.

'We'll help tidy things up!' said Lucy.

'Thank you,' said Rosie's mum. 'I'm afraid I think we might need a magic wand to tidy up this farm!

Or a magic snow globe, thought Lucy, remembering the special snow globe she had packed in her bag.

Anyway, let's not worry about that now. It's lovely to have you here, Lucy, and you Sita, of course.

This house is beautiful but it feels a bit big for just the four of us.'

Lucy's mum kissed Lucy goodbye, and then Lucy and Sita helped Rosie put up the paper chains and lay the table for dinner. They had pasta and tomato sauce and then the cakes Lucy's Gran had made. Leah's eyes kept closing and she nearly fell asleep at the table.

'Time for bed, young lady,' said Peter, and picked her up in his arms to go to bed. Leah kissed them each goodnight and then fell asleep again, her head on Peter's shoulder.

'She's so sweet!' said Lucy.

They went into the sitting room and played Monopoly and had lots of fun. The sitting room was lovely and cosy with a crackling log fire and a Christmas tree and lots of Christmas cards hanging up, but it was a bit strange when it was time to go upstairs to bed. Rosie's grandad hadn't used the upstairs for a while before he went into the home, and the room the girls were sleeping in was quite big and bare. Rosie had done her best, putting bright coloured blankets on the three camp beds, but Lucy suddenly really missed her own little bedroom and Merry and Rocky.

'I'm sorry it is so dark and bare up here,' said Rosie, looking worried. 'I thought it would be fun to have a sleepover in Grandad's house but now I'm not so sure.'

'Don't worry,' said Sita. 'The beds look so cosy!'

'It's fine!' said Lucy, 'And look what I brought too!' She took the snow globe out of her bag and switched the night light on. She put it on the floor by her bed and Scruffy on the pillow, and felt much better. Then she shook the snow globe to make the snow fall.

'It is so lovely!' said Sita. 'I could look at that for hours.'

The girls got into their pyjamas and brushed their teeth in the bathroom. When they came back into the room, Rosie's mum had put hot-water bottles in their beds so it was very warm and they snuggled down.

'I've got you both presents,' said Rosie. 'I know I could give them to you nearer Christmas but I just can't wait.'

Rosie passed them each a soft parcel.

Sita opened hers first. 'It's a pencil case in the shape of a dog!' she said. 'And it has lots of pens with my name on them.

Thanks, Rosie!'

'It's because you are going to get a puppy, and also to remind you to write to us lots!' said Rosie.

Lucy opened her present from Rosie—it was a soft toy donkey with long ears and legs and big brown eyes.

'Oh, Rosie—she is lovely! I'm going to call her Mistletoe! Thank you so much!' said Lucy as she cuddled the little donkey.

Lucy reached for Scruffy and gave them a hug together. 'Look—you can be friends,' she whispered, and she could almost see Scruffy's tail wag. Lucy knew Rocky and Merry would love Mistletoe too.

'I got you a toy donkey because I know how much you love donkeys,' said Rosie.

'I can't wait to see Pixie tomorrow!' said Lucy. 'It's so exciting Pixie is expecting a foal next year.'

If Pixie isn't rehomed soon, then the foal might come when she is here,' said Rosie. 'Mum has never looked after a donkey having a foal before but she says she is reading up all about it and knows when to call the vet if Pixie needs help.'

'I'd love to see the baby donkey,' said Sita. 'You've got to send me photos!'

When Rosie's mum switched off the light, Lucy made sure the snow globe was lit up and shook it again so that they could all see the snow falling on the house in the little wood.

'I'm so glad you brought it,' said Rosie. 'I might ask for a snow globe light for Christmas too. It's so pretty. Where did you get it, Lucy?'

'I don't know. I've always had it,' said
Lucy.

'I'm so glad you are both here,' said Rosie. 'Thank you for coming.'

'It makes you wonder who lives in the little house and what the little wood is like, doesn't it?' said Sita, sleepily, as they watched the snow fall and settle.

'Grandad has a little wood on his farm,' said Rosie, yawning. 'We got the logs for the fire from it. We can go and look at it tomorrow if you like.'

'We must go and see Pixie first, though,' said Lucy, giving Mistletoe a kiss on the top of her head.

Lucy lay awake for a little after the others fell asleep. She could see the

43

stars through a chink in the curtains. She was warm and cosy, and with her friends, and she wasn't scared of the dark any more. She could hear the others sleeping as she cuddled Mistletoe and Scruffy and looked at her snow globe.

Lucy leant over and shook the globe once more.

'I wish there was a way to keep the farm going,' she whispered. 'And I wish I could go inside the globe and visit the little house and wood.' And at that moment, everything changed.

Chapter Four

Inside the globe the door of the little
cottage opened and out came two tiny
figures—Santa, all dressed in red, and
a tiny white baby reindeer. Santa looked
up and waved.

Suddenly it was snowing in the

room, so heavily that Lucy couldn't see the others in their beds. She didn't feel scared or worried though, just excited. Something wonderful was happening.

'I'm having such a lovely dream,' she said. She sat up and put out her hands and felt the snowflakes fall on them. She put out her tongue and felt one land on it. 'It all feels so real,' she said to herself.

'Lucy!' she heard a deep voice call through the blizzard. It was familiar and kind, and it made her feel happy and fizzy inside. Then suddenly two little hooves were on her bed and a sweet little white reindeer with sparkling fur was snuffling and butting his head against her.

'Starlight!' said the deep voice with a chuckle. 'Let Lucy get out of bed!' And through the snow came the figure of Santa with his red coat and trousers and a long white beard.

He wasn't small like he was in the snow globe any more.

'Santa!' said Lucy, and jumped out of bed and flung her arms around him. His red coat was soft and warm and smelt of cinnamon and woodsmoke. The little reindeer ran in excited circles around them.

'Starlight is so excited you have come to visit us in the snow globe at last!' laughed Santa. 'He has been waiting for

you to make that wish! Come on—let's bring Scruffy and Mistletoe too, shall we?'

Lucy turned back to get the toys from the bed, but the bed wasn't there any more. Instead, she was standing barefoot in a wood, and it was snowing, and a little white reindeer and a brown and white dog and a tiny long-legged donkey foal were chasing each other through the trees.

'You love them, so they are welcome here!' said Santa, beaming. 'Look who else has come this special night!'

Lucy heard a soft whinny and turned to see Rocky, no longer on his rockers, but a pretty little brown pony. Curled up on his back was a little ginger cat.

'Rocky! I can't believe you are here!' said Lucy, and patted his neck. He tossed his head and snorted gently, his eyes brown and kind.

'Hello, Merry!' said Lucy, and she picked the little cat up and cuddled her.

Scruffy and Mistletoe charged up to Rocky, and they all ran excitedly off into the woods.

'Don't worry,' said Santa. 'They will be safe in my woods, and when they are tired they can come in and get warm.'

Starlight stayed with Lucy and butted his head against her, his little reindeer tail wagging with happiness.

'You really are the sweetest little reindeer in the world!' said Lucy, giving him a hug.

'Come inside!' said Santa. 'Welcome to our cottage in the woods!'

He opened the door and knocked his boots against the mat so that the snow fell off. Lucy looked down at her bare feet and suddenly shivered and felt cold for the first time.

'Now, go inside and get warm on the sofa over there by the fire,' said Santa. Merry ran in front of her to curl up in front of a roaring wood fire, the bright flames flickering as the smoke went up the chimney. It was a big room, like the farmhouse kitchen, and full of colourful books and pictures and toys and musical instruments.

There was a comfortable deep red sofa in front of the fire with green cushions, and Lucy went to sit on it. Santa put a lovely thick coloured patchwork blanket, a bit like the ones Rosie had put on their beds, around her. It covered her cold feet as she snuggled into it so she felt warm again. The little white reindeer jumped up on the sofa and cuddled up close to her.

'You're like a little hot-water bottle, Starlight!' laughed Lucy, and flung her arms around him.

Santa had left the door half open, and Mistletoe decided to run in out of the snow. She was so excited that she had to run around and around the sofa a few times. Her little tail wagged and her long ears twitched and she made excited little *he-haws* as she went. Mistletoe was running so fast that she even got her legs a bit mixed up and she tripped over, but she didn't hurt herself—she just got up straight away and ran around a bit more until she got tired. She was so happy.

'Good girl, Mistletoe,' said Santa, smiling down at the little foal. 'Your donkey coat isn't waterproof like a horse's, so it's important you have shelter. Lie down whilst I make Lucy some cocoa, and then I'll show you the nice warm stable. I expect Rocky has found his way there already. He normally does.'

'Has Rocky been here before then?' said Lucy.

'Oh, often!' laughed Santa. 'But he only comes for visits when you are asleep because he loves being with you. So does Scruffy. You are so kind and they feel very loved by you.'

Lucy felt very proud and beamed at Santa. The little brown and white dog ran in, panting, his tail wagging. He came and gave Lucy a lick and then went and lay down next to Merry.

Mistletoe was very interested in Starlight and got up from where she had been lying. She walked up to the little reindeer and nuzzled him. Starlight nuzzled her back, but he didn't want to leave Lucy's arms, and Lucy was glad. Cuddling him was making her feel happy and warm inside from top to toe, and she loved the way his fur twinkled and sparkled the more she hugged him.

'Nobody gives cuddles the way you do!' chuckled Santa. 'You are just what Starlight needs before we go on our long journey delivering all the presents. He shows all the other reindeers the way and helps the sleigh go in the right direction, so he needs to be all filled up with love before we set off!'

Santa gave Lucy a mug full of hot chocolate. It had a picture of a tiny harvest mouse on it.

'How funny!' said Lucy. 'I was talking about harvest mice with Oscar. I wish they still lived in the fields near us.'

'I know,' said Santa, smiling. 'Now,

tell me about all the other things you wish for, Lucy.'

'Well,' said Lucy. 'I wish I could help save Rosie's grandad's farm. It's all overgrown and Rosie's mum and Peter her stepdad don't have the money to sort it out. It would make them and Rosie's grandad so sad to have to sell it. I wish I could help them.'

'Hmm,' said Santa. 'That's a very kind wish, Lucy. Now, drink up your hot chocolate, and I will give you some warm things to put on. Then I will take you to see my little wood and the creatures living in it.'

Lucy didn't feel cold at all when she went outside wearing the lovely red coat and hat and gloves and black boots Santa gave her. Rocky was waiting for her and gave a little whinny.

'I love you too,' said Lucy as Rocky gently nuzzled her. Rocky then walked ahead with little Mistletoe, who was now wearing a little green blanket with a picture of mistletoe on it on her back.

Starlight and Scruffy walked together beside Lucy and Santa. Merry started following, but mewed a little when snow got on her paws.

'Go home and keep my armchair warm, Merry,' said Santa. 'Lucy will be back for you soon!'

Merry rubbed herself against Lucy's leg and then happily went back into the house. Merry liked a warm fire more than a walk in the snow, but Lucy couldn't wait to go and see the little wood she had looked at for so long in the snow globe. This was going to be the most magical walk ever!

Chapter Five

The animals and birds came out of their nests and hollows and dens to greet Santa and Lucy as they walked around the wood and stopped in a moonlit clearing.

There were little rabbits hopping around everywhere, having lots of fun, but also little badgers and foxes, and they were playing together. They all ran to her, and Lucy found herself stroking and cuddling them in a way she would never do at the Wildlife Rescue Centre. They weren't frightened in the least and were so soft and snuffly and pleased to see her. A tawny owl flew down and sat on Santa's shoulder, and a red-breasted robin came and sang on a branch in the moonlight.

But there were other animals too— animals Lucy did not expect. Tiny multicoloured birds soared in a cloud above her head and then flew off again, their wings sounding like tiny bells as they flew. There was a flash of silver and then, out from behind the trees, into the clearing came a shy and beautiful unicorn who bowed its head before Santa.

'Beyond the wood I have many other homes for many other creatures: mountain homes, ocean homes, desert homes,' said Santa. 'The jewel birds and the unicorn live furthest away, but they came to the wood today because they heard how kind you are and they wanted to see you.'

The shy silver-white unicorn stayed, and she and Rocky seemed to be particularly pleased to see each other.

'They are old friends,' said Santa.

Lucy watched as they galloped around together, tossing their heads and their manes. Starlight and Mistletoe looked so sweet when they tried to copy them.

'This is so wonderful!' said Lucy to Santa. 'It is just what I wished for!'

'Now Lucy,' said Santa. 'Come with me. I especially want to show you a little animal who lives in the fields by the wood.'

They walked through the wood until

they came out of the trees to a bare winter field, with grass growing high at the edges. The night was bright with the light of the moon.

Santa bent down. 'This little creature will have heard our footsteps through the ground already, but because he knows the sound of my feet, he will run up to see me. I think you will want to meet him! Come out, little harvest mouse!' Santa called, and up out of the grass darted a tiny reddish-brown little mouse with little ears and a long tail. It ran onto Santa's hand and curled its tail around his thumb as he lifted it up to show Lucy.

'Here he is, Lucy,' said Santa.

The little mouse on Santa's hand gazed at Lucy with its dark little eyes and twitched its whiskers.

'You're lovely!' said Lucy.

'Thank you!' laughed Sita.

Lucy opened her eyes. She was lying in bed, cuddling Scruffy and Mistletoe, and wearing her pyjamas.

'You were talking in your sleep,' said Rosie.

Lucy looked around. She was at a sleepover with Rosie and Sita, not in Santa's magic snow globe. The snow globe was on the floor beside her bed, with its little wood and cottage, Scruffy and Mistletoe were sweet little toys, not magical animals at all, and there was no tiny mouse to be seen.

'I had such a wonderful dream!' she said.

'Well, now it's time to get out of bed and come down and have a lovely breakfast!' said Rosie.

The girls put on their dressing gowns andslippersandwentdownstairs.Leahwas up already and very pleased to see them.

Rosie's mum was a brilliant cook. She had made fresh bread which smelt and tasted so good with butter and homemade jam.

'Time to go and see Pixie!' said Rosie.

'Race you to get dressed!' And she and Sita and Lucy rushed upstairs to get ready.

'That dream seemed so real,' said Lucy to herself as she brushed her teeth. 'I feel as if I really have met Santa and Starlight before. I wonder if my wishes will come true.'

'Come on, slow coach!' called Rosie outside the bathroom door. 'Pixie is waiting.'

'Coming!' said Lucy, putting her toothbrush back in her bag. Staying with Rosie might not be a dream, but it was exciting too. She couldn't wait to go to the stable to see the donkey.

Pixie was a very gentle animal. She came slowly towards the girls and let them pat her neck. She bent her head and Lucy felt her soft ears. Then the girls let her out into the field whilst

they cleared out the dirty straw from the stable and put some fresh hay in the manger, some donkey pellets in the feeding trough, and clean water in the water bucket.

Pixie took her time to come back in, and she had a bit of mud on her back when she did. 'She loves rolling on the ground,' said Rosie. 'But she does get in a mess.'

Pixie wasn't interested in eating the new hay. She let Rosie gently brush the mud away but then walked off, as if to say, 'That's enough.'

'Perhaps she isn't hungry. Her tummy is very round,' said Sita.

'I expect that's because she is expecting a foal,' said Lucy.

They went back in to wash their hands and have some of Rosie's mum's mince pies.

'Your mum is such a good cook!' said Sita. 'My mum says she will miss her cooking—she says she makes better cakes than the teashops in town.'

'Hey—what about my flapjack biscuits?' said Peter, laughing, as he came in with Lucy's dad and Oscar and Gran. 'They are pretty good too, I'll have you know!'

'Hello, Dad and Oscar and Gran!' said Lucy. 'Why are you all here?'

'Peter says we can all go to the wood and choose a Christmas tree each for us and Gran and maybe pick some holly,' said Oscar.

'And we'll choose another for Rosie's grandad's home,' said Peter. 'He will be coming to spend Christmas Day with us, but it will be nice for the home to have a real tree, and we can all help decorate it.'

'It's a little walk,' said Rosie's mum, 'so we should really get going now. I've put some jacket potatoes on and by the time we get back your mum and your dad, Sita, should be here too and we can all have some lunch together.'

'Then we can make decorations for

the trees!' said Rosie. 'Do you want to make a Christmas fairy for the top of our tree, Leah?'

'No,' said Leah, shaking her head. 'I want to make a Christmas mouse.'

'Can you wait a minute?' said Lucy, and she rushed upstairs and put the snow globe in the deep pocket of her winter coat. She didn't know why, but she had a feeling she would need it.

Chapter Six

It was fun walking to the woods, but it was very clear that the farm was in trouble. Once they got past the donkey field things were overgrown, with broken fences and ivy and nettles.

Peter put Leah on his shoulders so she wouldn't get stung, and Lucy could hear Rosie's mum saying to Lucy's mum and Gran, 'I know that someone wants to buy the farm next door too because the old lady who owns it lives in the home with Dad, and her daughter visits her. Someone keeps asking her to sell so they can build on it. Maybe we should sell too. We just don't have the time or money to run it. But it seems such a shame if it will be built over.'

'What a lovely little wood!' said Prajit when they got there. 'What are the trees they have here?'

'Mainly sweet chestnut, oak, and silver birch,' said Oscar. 'Although, if we are collecting some Christmas trees you must have some conifers. What?' he said as everybody looked at him, surprised.

'I'm just surprised! I thought you were our footballing, not our tree expert!' said Dad, and he and Prajit laughed.

'Why can't I know a bit about trees too?' said Oscar crossly. 'I got a book about trees for Christmas last year and I've been reading it. What's the problem?'

He went red and stomped off angrily ahead of them.

'Oh dear,' said Lucy's mum.

'Oscar is right,' said Gran. 'This bit is wonderful—it is ancient woodlands. You can see your grandad coppiced it, Rosie, the way that people have been doing for hundreds of years, cutting trees down in different places and letting the plants and insects have space to thrive. Ancient woodlands are perfect for wildlife.'

'The conifers are in a separate little area on one side of the wood,' said Rosie's mum. 'My dad only started growing them ten years ago to see if he could sell them at Christmas time, but then my mum got ill and he ended up just giving the trees to friends.'

Sita, Lucy, and Rosie walked ahead.

'Your brother went so red,' said Sita.

'I know. He hates it when he thinks people are laughing at him,' said Lucy.

'Well, so do I,' said Rosie. 'Poor Oscar.'

'I'll go and see if he is OK,' said Lucy 'but he might just be cross with me too.'

Oscar was still embarrassed and a bit grumpy when Lucy caught up with him. They were at the edge of the ancient bit of the wood by then, beside a field.

'I didn't know you knew all about trees,' she said.

'Why shouldn't I?' said Oscar crossly, but Lucy could see he felt really hurt. 'I wish people would listen to me more and stop laughing. I don't just like playing football—I know about other things too. And it isn't just you who likes animals. I wish people would know that too.'

Lucy felt the snow globe grow warm in her pocket and looked down.

'What have you got in your pocket?' said Oscar. 'Lucy! Why have you got your snow globe on the walk?'

Suddenly, a little white deer with sparkling fur ran across the path in front of them, out on to the edge of the wood, and disappeared just by the tall grass by the field. Lucy thought she saw a trail of stars which glittered and then vanished,

and that she heard the sound of tinkling bells, but she couldn't be sure.

Oscar's mouth dropped open. 'Lucy! Did you see that? It must have been a trick of the light, but I thought I saw something run into the long grass.' He shook his head. 'It reminded me of a dream I once had. About a magic reindeer and Christmas.'

Lucy wasn't sure if Oscar would believe her if she told him that he had really seen Starlight, Santa's reindeer, but she didn't have time to say anything anyway. Oscar walked carefully into the long grass and the next moment gave an excited shout.

'Dad! Gran! Lucy! Look!'

Everyone came running to see what Oscar had found. He was beaming, holding up a little ball of brown grass.

'What's that?' said Lucy's dad.

'It's an old harvest mouse nest, isn't it, Gran?' said Oscar.

'It is! Well done, Oscar!' said Gran. 'Let's have a look around and see if we can find any more.'

Oscar quickly found another nearby.

'This is marvellous news!' said Gran, beaming. 'The way the grass at the edge of the field has been left to grow has meant that harvest mice are safely living here. They must have used

85

those nests last spring.'

'Well, I am very impressed that Oscar recognized a harvest mouse nest when he saw it,' said Joanna, Sita's mum.

'So am I,' said Lucy's dad. 'Well done, son! I'm sorry I laughed at you earlier. I'm proud you knew what the trees were.'

'I'm sorry too,' said Prajit. 'You'll have to teach us more about them.'

Lucy's dad put his arm across Oscar's shoulders and gave him a hug. Oscar looked very happy.

Lucy put her hand in her pocket and touched the snow globe, now cool again. 'Thank you, snow globe, thank you, Starlight,' she said quietly. For a minute the globe grew warm again, so she knew her thanks had been heard.

Everyone had a lot of fun choosing the Christmas trees. They cut three small ones down and then, in pairs, Oscar and Lucy's dad, Prajit and Peter, and Joanna and Lucy's mum took a small tree each and carried them, huffing and puffing a little, back through the wood to the farmhouse. Lucy and Rosie and Sita walked with Gran and Leah, and when Leah got a bit tired the girls took it in turns to give her a piggyback all the way home.

Everyone stayed for lunch. After the meal everyone left except for Lucy and Sita. They were staying a second night at the sleepover, much to Leah's delight.

'We can make some decorations for the Christmas trees this afternoon,' said Rosie. 'We'll make enough so that we can bring them to put on the tree at Grandad's home and the one at your Gran's Wildlife Rescue Centre tomorrow.'

They had lots of fun making tiny little clay animals to hang on the branches and painting them. Lucy made a tiny harvest mouse especially for Leah. Leah was so happy she gave Lucy a big hug and a kiss, and played with her little mouse all the rest of the afternoon. Lucy made little jewel birds and a silver unicorn as well.

Sita made two kangaroos. 'You can each have one for your trees and think of me every Christmas,' she said.

Rosie made three donkeys: one each.

'I don't want us to leave the farm,' she said sadly. 'Especially now I know the wood is so ancient and special, and we have harvest mice. But most of all, I don't want to leave Pixie. I love her so much.'

'Don't worry,' said Lucy. 'We'll think of a way for you to save the farm and the wood.'

'How?' said Sita.

'I don't know,' said Lucy, but she thought of the snow globe upstairs by her bed, and she remembered telling her wish to Santa. 'I just have a feeling that soon everything will change.'

Chapter Seven

After dinner the girls watched a Christmassy film before bed, and Rosie practised singing 'Little Donkey' for the concert the next day at Forest Lodge, the old people's home her grandad was in. Lucy and Sita clapped when she finished, and Rosie beamed.

'I feel so much better about singing than last year,' she said. 'I really hope Grandad enjoys it.'

They went upstairs and told each other jokes. Then Sita got out pens from her pencil case and they played a funny game where, on folded paper, without knowing what the others had drawn, one of them drew a head, one drew a body, and one drew feet. They ended up with some very strange creatures indeed. Then they played consequences where they each wrote the beginning and middle and end of a story. One of the stories went:

Once Lucy was walking in a wood.

Lucy met Santa.

And Rosie's farm was saved.

'I wish that was true,' said Rosie a bit sadly, 'especially now we know we have harvest mice.'

Lucy looked quickly over at the snow globe. The snow had started falling again, and she knew she hadn't shaken it.

Sita leant over and picked up the snow globe. 'I wish I had a snow globe like this, Lucy,'

'Me too,' said Rosie.

'I really wish as well that I could see

Pixie's foal before we go,' added Sita. 'We will be in Australia for New Year. I'm really looking forward to seeing Gran and Gramps and my old friends and my school, and I'm looking forward to my new puppy, but I'll miss you two so much.'

She shook the globe and put it down before getting into bed. Lucy didn't say anything, but she was sure she could see, in the snow globe, behind the falling snow, a thin line of smoke rising from the chimney of the little house in the woods.

'Was that a dream, or was I really

there?' Lucy thought. She looked down
at Mistletoe and Scruffy, lying beside
her in the bed. It was hard to imagine
them running around the wood, but as
she looked, Lucy was almost sure she
could see one of Mistletoe's soft furry

ears twitch, and Scruffy's tail give a little wag. She suddenly felt very, very happy inside, as if she had been given some good news. The funny thing was, she didn't really know what it was yet. 'I just know it is all going to be all right,' said Lucy to herself, and felt very sleepy and peaceful inside.

Rosie's mum had put hot-water bottles in their beds again, and the girls had put paper chains and tinsel up so it all looked so much nicer than the first night. The girls snuggled down.

'Good night' said Rosie, switching off the light and climbing back into bed. The curtains were closed and the only light came from the snow globe, the snow still falling steadily as the girls slept.

Lucy was woken by soft long ears tickling her. She sat up in the dark. Sitting on the patchwork quilt, looking at her, was Mistletoe the baby donkey. Scruffy was still a cuddly pyjama case, but Mistletoe was alive the way she had been in the snow globe, her soft fur glowing with magic. Mistletoe ran back down to the foot of the bed and looked back, as if to make sure Lucy was following her. Then she leapt off the bed and landed in a bit of a muddle on the floor.

'Mistletoe! Are you OK?' whispered Lucy, clambering to the end of the bed and looking down. Mistletoe looked up, her big eyes shining, and got up to her feet again, her little tail whisking from side to side. She ran and stood by the door as if waiting for Lucy to open it. Lucy got out of bed, pushed her feet into her slippers and got into her dressing gown.

'I'm coming,' she said softly, and opened the door to the landing. The tiny donkey foal stood at the top of the stairs, looking uncertainly down.

'Do you want to go down them?' said Lucy. 'I'll carry you, Mistletoe.' Lucy picked her up—Mistletoe was warm and fluffy and soft and gave Lucy

a loving little nuzzle and a soft donkey bray. As soon as they got to the bottom of the stairs Mistletoe wriggled so much Lucy put her down, and off she ran across the kitchen and stood by the garden door.

'Do you want me to go out into the garden?' said Lucy. She pulled the bolt back and turned the big key and opened the door. Lucy felt something soft falling on her face.

'It's snowing!' she said. 'Sita will be so pleased. We are going to have a white Christmas!'

Lucy followed Mistletoe as she ran down the path towards the donkey shelter and field, and as they got nearer she heard the sound of Pixie braying. She couldn't see very well in the dark, but she knew something was wrong. Pixie was in pain. Lucy could feel her heart beating fast.

'Do you want me to get help?' she said to Mistletoe. The little donkey nodded and ran back up the path, into the kitchen, and stood at the bottom of the stairs, looking up. Lucy went to pick her up but she disappeared in a cloud of stars, so Lucy ran upstairs as fast as she could and banged on Rosie's mum's door to tell them what she had heard, and Rosie's mum and Peter ran down with a torch to check on Pixie. Lucy stayed in the kitchen. Peter was back very quickly.

'Well done, Lucy!' he said. 'Pixie's foal is coming sooner than we expected, and Pixie is in trouble. I think she needs some help. The vet is on her way over right now. Thank you so much. I don't know what we would have done if you hadn't heard Pixie. Go back to bed now and I'll tell you all about it in the morning.'

Lucy went back up to bed. She felt very worried about Pixie, and as soon as she got up to the bedroom she picked up the snow globe. It wasn't snowing any more, but the little world in the wood looked calm and peaceful.

'I know you are a magic Christmas snow globe, and I really need your help,' she whispered, trying not to cry. 'I am so worried about Pixie. Please can she be OK and have a lovely little donkey foal.'

To Lucy's surprise, as soon as she had

said those words, the door of the snow globe's little cottage opened and Santa and Starlight came out. Santa stood and waved up at her, and Starlight gave a little jump. Then Santa gave her another wave, and put his two thumbs up as if to say everything would be fine, and then they both went back in. The snow globe looked as it always did. But Lucy felt comforted.

She looked over at Mistletoe lying next to Scruffy on the bed. The little donkey was a cuddly toy again. But Lucy noticed there was a trace of snow on her little hooves.

'Thank you, Mistletoe,' she said quietly. 'I think Santa sent you to get help for Pixie. I'm so glad you are my little donkey now, and I know I saw Santa and Starlight in the globe. They will make sure everything works out.'

Lucy reached over to give Mistletoe a cuddle and as she fell asleep with her in her arms, Lucy was sure she heard a soft donkey bray and felt a loving little donkey nuzzling her goodnight.

Chapter Eight

'Did I dream all that?' thought Lucy to herself as she woke up the next morning and saw Mistletoe and Scruffy lying in the bed next to her. She didn't say anything to Rosie and Sita, but when they went downstairs for breakfast and saw Rosie's mum there with a big smile on her face, then she knew everything had really happened.

'Girls! Pixie has had her foal! She had a few problems, but luckily Lucy heard her and told us so we got the vet, and now everything is absolutely fine.'

'Lucy!' said Rosie. 'Why didn't you say?'

'I thought I had dreamt it,' laughed Lucy.

'So my wish has come true!' said Sita happily.

'It's a little girl foal—she's so sweet,' said Rosie's mum. 'If you eat your breakfast up and get dressed you can come and see her. Pixie may be a bit protective of her foal so we must be careful and I just want you to peep at her today. The vet did say it would be good for the foal to see people early on, so you must come often over Christmas. I am glad we are bringing Grandad home today, Rosie. I feel like we need to have an expert here to advise us!'

The girls rushed their breakfast and went and stood very quietly at the door of the stable. A gorgeous fluffy little soft grey donkey foal was standing unsteadily on her feet, her legs looking very long for her body, her ears and head very big.

'Hello,' said Lucy softly, and the little donkey looked back at Lucy and gazed at her for a minute with her beautiful big eyes, as if she knew how much Lucy had helped her. It made Lucy feel happy deep down inside. Then the little foal put her head down and started drinking milk from her mum. Pixie stood at the back of the stable and looked calmly over at the girls. She didn't seem to mind them looking over at her.

'She is so beautiful,' said Rosie sadly as they walked back to the house. 'I can't bear to think that Grandad will have to sell the farm if we can't make it work. If we go back to our old house then our garden by the river is too small for donkeys. They will have to be re-homed and Pixie has only just come here.'

'Look—don't worry,' said Lucy. 'You have the concert at the old people's home this afternoon and we promised to make biscuits for the party. Let's make lots of biscuits now and you practise singing some more, and maybe by the end of the day we will have some brilliant idea to save the farm.'

'Oh, Lucy,' said Rosie, and gave her a hug.

Sita and Lucy did their best to cheer up Rosie the rest of the morning. They made lots of biscuits and listened to Rosie practise. In between all of this they went back and forth to peek at the little foal, who was getting steadier and steadier on her feet and looking fluffier and sweeter each time they saw her. Pixie looked very happy to be a mum.

Halfway through the morning the vet came and checked on Pixie and the foal.

'They are doing very well,' she said, smiling at the girls as she went out. 'It was good I was called out last night to help, but now there should be no more problems.'

Lucy was sure Santa had sent Mistletoe to tell her that Pixie was in trouble.

'Thank you Santa,' she whispered.

They took the biscuits out of the oven and left them cooling on racks. Sita had made ginger biscuits, Rosie had made chocolate biscuits, and Lucy cinnamon biscuits. Then they all had cheese toasties for lunch and got ready to go to the concert. Lucy's and Sita's families were going to meet them there.

When they arrived, Oscar and Lucy's mum and dad were already there. Oscar was sitting chatting to Rosie's grandad and looking very happy.

'I'm very impressed with this lad,' said Rosie's grandad to Rosie's mum as they came in. 'He knows a lot about wildlife. He has been telling me about all the harvest mice nests he found on the farm.'

'Excuse me, did you say harvest mice?' said a voice. Lucy recognized the lady who was talking—it was the vet who had visited Pixie and her foal.

'Yes,' said Oscar. 'It looks like there are harvest mice nesting on Rosie's grandad's farm.'

'My name is Nieve O'Connor—I came to see your donkey and her foal last night. Rosie's grandad's farm is the farm next to yours, Mum,' said Nieve the vet to her mum.

'This means that there must be lots of land where weedkiller hasn't been used and where there is still grass and other plants for them to nest in safely.'

'There's plenty of that,' said Rosie's grandad. 'I haven't been able to work the land as much as I wanted to these last years.'

'We've been meaning to buy weedkiller but it has been so expensive we haven't been able to afford it yet,' said Peter.

'I've got the same problem,' said Nieve's mum, sitting next to him.

'That's not a problem—that's great news!' said Nieve. 'That means that there must be lots of wildlife living safely on both your land!'

'The trouble is that I don't know how we can carry on running the farm,' said Rosie's mum. 'We don't really have

enough money to keep it going.'

Rosie and Sita and Lucy looked at each other.

'We have got to think of an idea to make the money we need!' said Rosie. 'We must save the farm and keep Pixie and her foal'

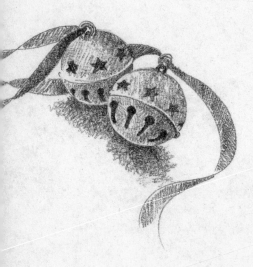

Chapter Nine

It was time for Rosie to sing her solo.
She sang the carol 'Litttle Donkey' so
beautifully that everyone clapped and
her grandad had to wipe happy tears
from his eyes. Leah got very excited and

wanted to sing it again, so then everyone at the concert—the people who lived there, and their visitors and the nurses and staff—all sang it a second time together.

Then Lucy's gran came in with a trolley with tea and the biscuits and cakes she and the girls had made. The girls and Oscar helped pass them around to everyone.

'These biscuits are absolutely delicious!' said Nieve the vet.

'And I love this cake!' said another visitor.

'You should open a café!' said someone else.

'That's it!' said Lucy, excitedly. 'A café! And we can run it!'

'What do you mean, Lucy?' said her mum.

'Well, you make such lovely soup and bread, and Rosie's mum loves cooking so much, and we can all make biscuits too. The farmhouse is so big and beautiful, we can have a café in it, and people can buy food and come and see the donkeys. We can save other donkeys too. The rest of the fields and the wood can be for wild animals and birds to live safely, and as places for people to walk and cycle without traffic!' said Lucy, beaming

'Do you know,' said Gran, 'I think

that's a brilliant idea! My friend had to close their donkey sanctuary, so it would be wonderful to open one at the farm.'

'I definitely think we should do this,' said Peter, smiling.

'I think that Mum and I would love to see if we can help—we'd rather the land be used like this than sold to be built on,' said Nieve the vet.

'I agree!' said her mum. 'It would break my heart to see the land go.'

'Well,' said Rosie's mum, 'if we sell our old house we can get the café started and open the farm and the land to the public. I really think it could work!'

'This is going to be the most

wonderful Christmas ever!' said Rosie, and she and Lucy and Sita gave each other a big excited hug.

On Christmas Eve, Lucy, back in her own bedroom, snuggled down in her bed with Mistletoe and Scruffy. Merry was curled up against her back, purring loudly, and Rocky was standing by the window. Beside her the snow globe glowed gently.

'Thank you for making all our wishes come true,' Lucy said sleepily. 'Tomorrow Sita and her family are coming for Christmas lunch and then we are all going over to Rosie's to see them and Pixie and her little foal. Rosie says Sita can name her before she goes. Everyone is so excited as the harvest mice have come back, and, did you know, Rosie's grandad is so happy the farm is saved and that he will be able to visit it lots.

Gran and I even found snow globes for Rosie and Sita at the Christmas market, so they will get lovely surprises tomorrow when they open their presents. I wonder if their snow globes will be as magical as you?'

There was a sound of tinkling bells far off, and Lucy saw, through the window, a little flashing light travelling across the sky.

'Good luck, Santa and Starlight,' she whispered. 'Thank you for the most magical Christmas surprise ever—a new home for wild animals and donkeys to be safe in. And Happy Christmas!'

Thank you . . .

to my lovely husband Graeme and my
children Joanna, Michael, Laura
and Christina, for all their support
and love.

To my dogs Timmy and Ben, who keep
me company whilst I write.

A special thank you to my kind
neighbour Emma Haynes, who took me
to see the donkeys at The Lord Whisky
Sanctuary in Kent, and to the lovely
staff there who answered
my questions.

And to my agent Anne Clark, the
wonderful illustrator Sophy Williams
and everyone at OUP for their
enthusiasm and hard work on and
for the Lucy books.

I love donkeys so much, and my
(not so secret) dream is to have some
of my own one day. Until then
I really enjoyed seeing them at
The Lord Whisky Sanctuary and
reading about them.

The Lord Whisky Sanctuary is a lovely
place which helps lots of animals.

http://www.lordwhisky.co.uk

I also love looking at this donkey
sanctuary website and have adopted
a donkey called Zena in the Sidmouth
Sanctuary In Devon. Even if I can't go
to visit her easily I can look at the
webcam and see if I can spot her!

www.thedonkeysanctuary.org.uk

About the author

Every Christmas, Anne used to ask for a dog. She had to wait many years, but now she has two dogs, called Timmy and Ben. Timmy is a big, gentle golden retriever who loves people and food and is scared of cats. Ben is a small brown and white cavalier King Charles spaniel who is a bit like a cat because he curls up in the warmest places and bosses Timmy about. He snuffles and snorts quite a lot and you can tell what he is feeling by the way he walks. He has a particularly pleased patter when he has stolen something he shouldn't have, which gives him away immediately. Anne lives in a village in Kent and is not afraid of spiders.

If you enjoyed

Lucy's Magical Surprise

then read on for a taster

of another of Lucy's festive

adventures,

Lucy's Winter Rescue

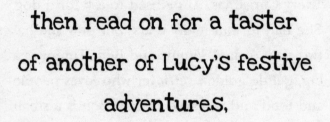

Chapter One

It was the week before Christmas, and Lucy and her friend Sita had gone to play at their friend Rosie's house for the afternoon.

It was always fun at Rosie's. She lived in a house by the river with her mum, and her stepdad, Peter. Peter and her mum had a little baby, so Rosie had a little sister, Leah. Everybody loved Leah. She was only two and a half and loved dressing up and playing with Rosie and her friends. Today Leah wanted to be Father Christmas's baby reindeer and live under the table, so the girls took it in turns to pretend to feed her and give her lots of special hugs. She was so sweet.

'Me baby rabbit now!' said Leah, coming out from under the table, jumping around the room.

'Leah would love my gran's Wildlife Rescue Centre!' laughed Lucy. 'We have a wild rabbit with a sore ear there now.'

'She'd love your uniform and the badges your gran makes for it too!' laughed Rosie. 'What animal badges have you got now?'

'Well, I've got badges for helping a magpie with a broken wing, and a newt, and we're looking after lots of tiny hedgehogs, so Gran is making me a hedgehog badge. I've got my rabbit badge already because of the little baby rabbit I rescued last Christmas.'

'That was when I had just arrived from Australia,' said Sita. 'I remember that little rabbit!'

'Me RABBIT!' shouted Leah.

'Why don't you be a sleeping bunny?' said Rosie, and she played a song on the piano about little bunnies being asleep.

'Everybody sleeping bunnies!' said Leah, and she made Lucy and Sita lie down beside her and pretend to be asleep. Leah looked very sweet and Lucy made Sita laugh by pretending to snore.

Then, when Rosie sang the waking up words 'Hop little bunny, hop, hop, hop!', Lucy and Sita had to jump up and down with Leah, who thought it was the best fun ever and kept hopping and hopping and laughing and laughing so that they all laughed too.

'Again! Again!' said Leah, but just at that moment, Rosie's mum came in.

'Thanks so much for playing with Leah, girls, but I think she might need a little nap now.'

'NO!' shouted Leah. 'Me bunny. Me HOP. Me not go bed.' Her face went very red and she started to cry.

'Girls—I don't think she will settle if

she thinks you are in the house. Do you think you could go and find some holly and ivy for me? I saw quite a lot growing next to the river the other day. I thought we might use it to help decorate the church for Christmas, and you can bring back some for your homes if you like. I'll give you some scissors and some thick gloves and this bag to put them in. Now girls, be careful not to get too near the river—it's got a lot higher lately. I think it's all the rain we've been having. I know you'll be sensible.'

The girls put on their warm coats and hats and scarves and went down Rosie's garden to her back gate and out on to

the wide path by the river. They could
still hear little Leah's wailing: 'No! No
sleep! Want GIRLS! Want DOGGY!'

'What does she mean?' said Sita. 'You
don't have a dog.'

'She keeps saying there's a dog in the garden,' said Rosie. 'But we've never seen one.'

'Poor Leah—she sounds so upset,' said Lucy.

'She'll be all right after her nap,' said Rosie, closing the gate behind her. 'She just got a bit too excited doing that song.'

'You're such a good singer,' said Sita.

'Um,' said Rosie, and made a face.

'What's the matter?' said Lucy.

'It's just that Mum and I are in the church choir, and we're going to sing carols at Forest Lodge—the old people's home my grandad's in. We're going to sing to them on Christmas Eve—and they want me to sing a solo.'

'That's great!' said Sita.

'You're so good at music! You'll be brilliant!' said Lucy.

Rosie bit her lip. 'I don't know—I'm just really worried. What if it all goes wrong and I let everyone down? Grandad has been telling everyone in the home about my singing. Mum and Peter say I will be fine, and even Dad is coming to see me. But what if I forget the words or sing out of tune? I'm so scared I keep having bad dreams and waking up and worrying about it.'

Just then Lucy heard a strange little cry coming from the riverbank—a faint, very high-pitched call, a bit like a cross between a whistle and a whimper.

'Did you hear that?' she said. A red breasted robin hopped on to a bush nearby and started singing.

'That's a robin,' said Sita. 'That's so Christmassy!'

'No, I meant the first noise. Listen. The girls stopped. The faint high noise came again, along with some tiny splashes.

'It's coming from those reeds on the riverbank near us,' said Lucy.

'Is it a water vole?' said Rosie. ' remember you told us Ratty in *The Wind in the Willows* was one.'

'I don't think it's a water vole,' said Lucy, turning in the direction of the cries and carefully making her way down the riverbank. 'I'd love to see one but Gran and I have looked and there are no burrows or droppings or tracks along this bit of the river. There are no feeding stations either, where they leave piles of stems of grass. But I think I may have an idea what it is. I think this animal is in *The Wind in the Willows* too. I just hope it isn't in trouble.'

'Be very careful,' said Rosie. 'Mum told us to stay away from the river.'

Lucy reached the riverbank, and peered into the reeds right at the edge. At first she could only see some rubbish—a crisp packet and a beer can—but then . . .

'Oh no!' said Lucy. 'This is awful. Can you pass me the gloves and the scissors, Rosie?'

Rosie and Sita carefully made their way down the bank to where Lucy was, and looked over her shoulder into the reeds. There, struggling to keep its head above the water, and trapped in the reeds, with some plastic rubbish around its neck, was a small furry animal.

'I was right—it's a baby otter!' said Lucy. 'I've never seen one so small. Gran told me they stay in their holt—that's their home—for about three months, so this one shouldn't be out alone at all. We've got to get it out of those reeds and keep it warm—look how it's shivering.'

'What should we do?' said Sita.

'I'm going to put on the thick gloves,' Lucy replied. 'It looks too tiny and weak to bite me but I'm not taking any chances: I know otter teeth are really sharp. Gran told me about a friend of hers who had to go to hospital when a grown–up otter bit her. Then I'm going to lift it out and hold it and you can cut the plastic off from around its neck.'

Lucy put on the gloves and lifted

the baby otter out. Lucy had learned from
her gran how to hold animals gently but
firmly so they couldn't bite. Sita carefully
cut the plastic off its neck. It was too weak

to struggle much and its poor little neck looked sore. Its fur was dark and sodden, and it was shivering.

'Here,' said Rosie, taking off her hat and scarf. 'Let's wrap it up and bring it home quickly. You can ring your gran from my house, Lucy.'

'It's very ill,' said Lucy, as they rushed back up the path. 'It might not even know how to swim yet—they don't learn until they are about ten weeks old and they are blind until they are four or five weeks old. Gran was teaching me about them last night. I didn't think I'd see one so soon. I wonder how old this one is.'

Back at Rosie's house, Lucy called

Gran and told her what they had found. Gran headed over straight away. Rosie found a cardboard box and a towel. They unwrapped the baby otter from Rosie's hat and scarf and tried to blot the excess water from its dark fur. It kept its eyes closed and didn't struggle.

'I'm so sorry girls, but it's very ill,' said Gran. 'It is so small—about nine weeks old—that I think the river water must have risen and washed this little cub out of its holt and downstream, and into the reeds and the rubbish. It shouldn't be outside yet. And it is so cold and that awful plastic has rubbed against its poor little neck and made it sore. I'll bring it back to the Centre now and I'll phone the vet. I think it will need an antibiotic injection to help it fight any infection it may have.'

Rosie and Sita looked upset. 'We're going to save it!' said Lucy confidently. 'I know we can. I'll go back with Gran now but I'll tell you all about it tomorrow—I promise.'

Lucy picked up the box and whispered, so that only the otter could hear. 'Don't worry—I have a magic snow globe and as soon as I get home I am going to wish on it for you. You'll be better for Christmas—I know you will!'

Reindeer Cupcakes

Makes 12

Before you start, you will need:

Equipment:
Mixing bowl
Wooden spoon
Sieve
12 Cupcake cases
Saucepan
Whisk
Spoon or spatula to
spread the icing
12 hole fairy cake tin

Ingredients:
125g butter, softened
175g caster sugar
2 eggs
200g self raising flour
100ml milk
100g dark chocolate
2 tbsp cocoa powder

For the chocolate icing:
50g dark chocolate
3 tbsp double cream

You will need an
adult to help you
with the oven
and melting the
chocolate for
the icing.

Method:

 Preheat the oven to 170C/325F/Gas 3.

 Set 12 cupcake cases on a baking sheet, equally spaced.

 In a large bowl, mix the butter and sugar together with a wooden spoon, until light and creamy.

 Gradually stir in the eggs and then sift the flour and cocoa into the bowl.

Break the chocolate up into small pieces, add to the saucepan and stir over a low heat until melted.

Mix in the milk and melted chocolate to your bowl.

Divide the mixture evenly into the cupcake cases.

 Put in the oven for 20-25 minutes. When they are ready, take out of the oven and place on a cooling rack.

When your cakes have cooled, you're ready for the fun part—decorating them!

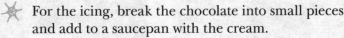

For the icing, break the chocolate into small pieces and add to a saucepan with the cream.

Stir over a low heat until all the chocolate has melted.

Spread the icing on top of the cupcakes.

You could use white chocolate drops for the reindeer's eyes, a red smartie or jelly tot for the nose, and chocolate buttons for the ears.

ANNE BOOTH

Can Lucy make
Starlight better and
save Christmas?

Lucy's Secret
REINDEER

ANNE BOOTH

Can Lucy save
Christmas for
a poorly rabbit?

Lucy's Magic
SNOW GLOBE

ANNE BOOTH

Christmas miracles
come in all sizes

Lucy's Winter
RESCUE